Book 2

Miss Annie
ROOFTOP CAT

Frank Le Gall
Illustrated by **Flore Balthazar**
Coloring by **Robin Doo**

Graphic Universe™ • Minneapolis • New York

Zeno's philosophical quote to Miss Annie on page 25 is part of Krishna's advice to Arjuna in the sacred Hindu book the *Bhagavad Gita*, which is part of the ancient Indian epic the *Mahabharata*.

Story by Frank Le Gall
Art by Flore Balthazar
Coloring by Robin Doo

Translation by Carol Klio Burrell

English translation copyright © 2012 by Lerner Publishing Group, Inc.

First American edition published in 2012 by Graphic Universe™. Published by arrangement with MEDIATOON LICENSING – France.

Miss Annie
© DUPUIS 2010 – Balthazar & Le Gall
www.dupuis.com

Graphic Universe™ is a trademark of Lerner Publishing Group, Inc.

Graphic Universe™
A division of Lerner Publishing Group, Inc.
241 First Avenue North
Minneapolis, MN 55401 U.S.A.

Website address: www.lernerbooks.com

Library of Congress Cataloging-in-Publication Data

Le Gall, Frank, 1959–
    Rooftop cat / by Frank Le Gall ; illustrated by Flore Balthazar.
        p.   cm. – (Miss Annie ; #2)
    Summary: Miss Annie, a young kitten, joins a group of cats in her neighborhood and, through their rivalry with other groups, learns about loyalty, courage, and the dangers of the world she is so eager to explore, helping her best mouse friend to become braver along the way.
    ISBN: 978-0-7613-7885-3 (lib. bdg. : alk. paper)
    1. Graphic novels. [1. Graphic novels. 2. Cats–Fiction. 3. Animals–Infancy–Fiction. 4. Mice–Fiction.] I. Balthazar, Flore, ill. II. Title.
PZ7.7.L42Roo 2012
741.5′973–dc23   2011025646

Manufactured in the United States of America
1 – DP – 12/31/11

1. At Night, All Cats Are Gray

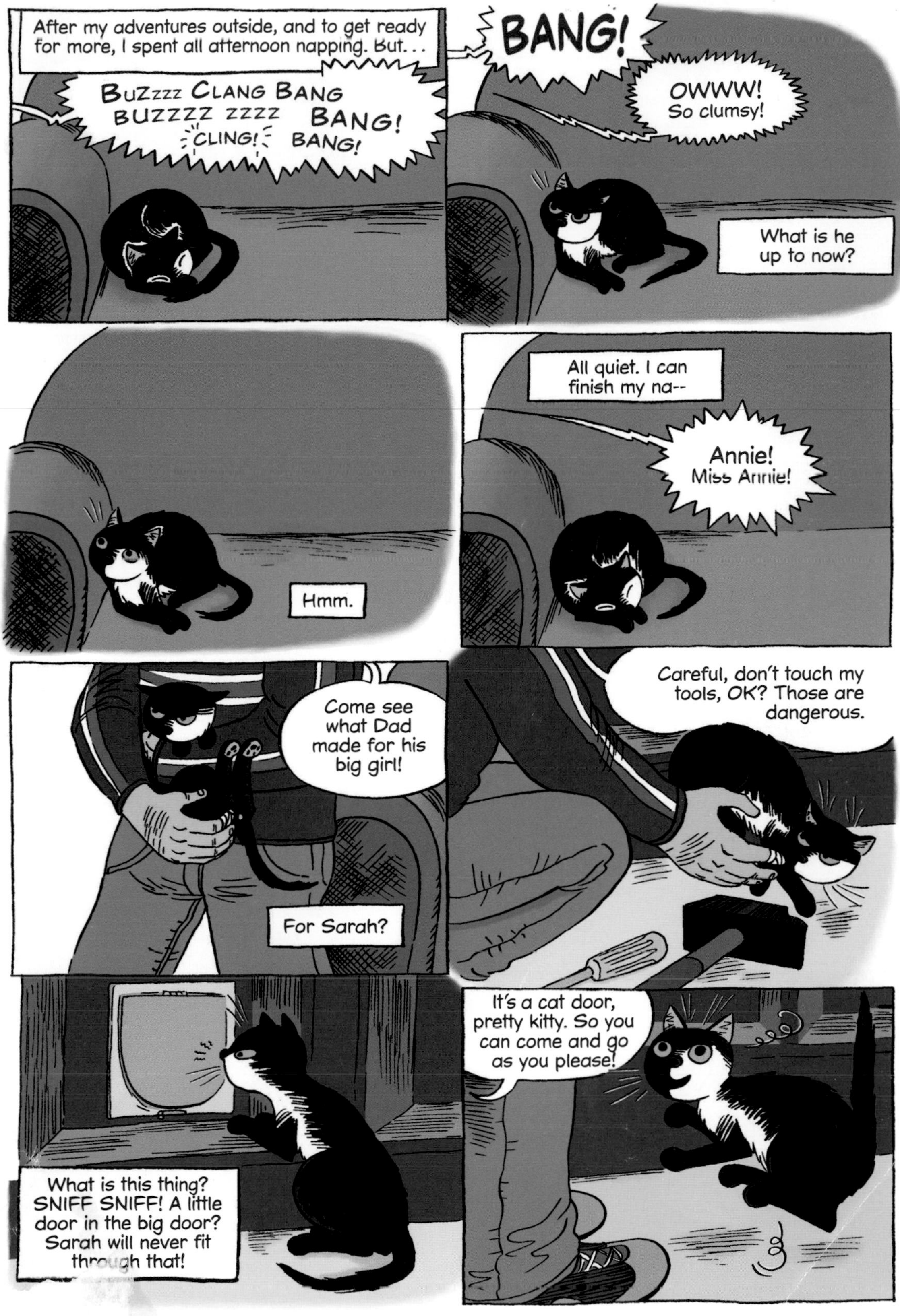
After my adventures outside, and to get ready for more, I spent all afternoon napping. But...
BuZzzz CLANG BANG BUZZZZ ZZZZ BANG! CLING! BANG!
BANG!
OWWW! So clumsy!
What is he up to now?
Hmm.
All quiet. I can finish my na--
Annie! Miss Annie!
Come see what Dad made for his big girl!
For Sarah?
Careful, don't touch my tools, OK? Those are dangerous.
What is this thing? SNIFF SNIFF! A little door in the big door? Sarah will never fit through that!
It's a cat door, pretty kitty. So you can come and go as you please!

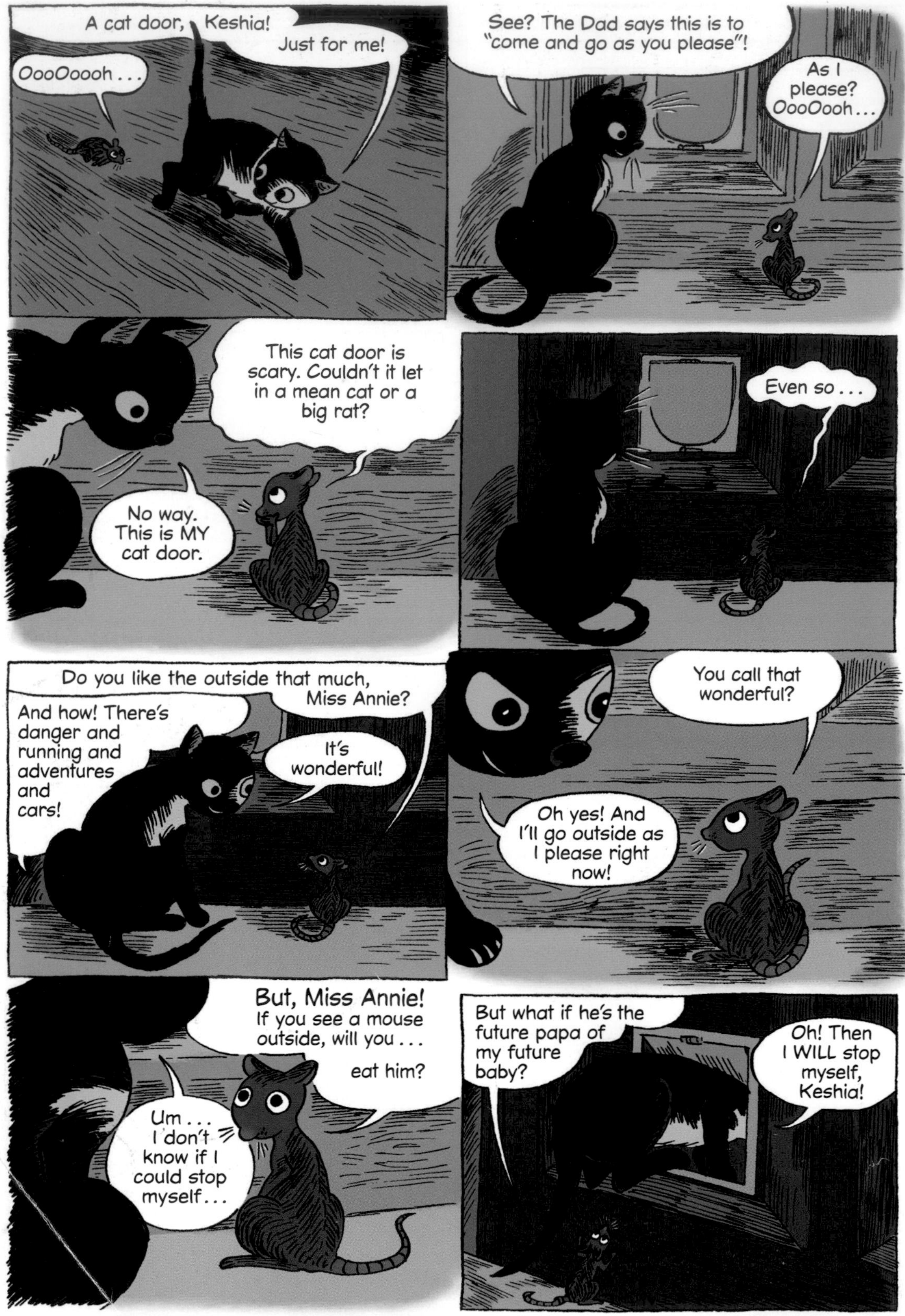
A cat door, Keshia!
Just for me!
OooOoooh . . .
See? The Dad says this is to "come and go as you please"!
As I please? OooOooh . . .
This cat door is scary. Couldn't it let in a mean cat or a big rat?
No way. This is MY cat door.
Even so . . .
Do you like the outside that much, Miss Annie?
And how! There's danger and running and adventures and cars!
It's wonderful!
You call that wonderful?
Oh yes! And I'll go outside as I please right now!
But, Miss Annie! If you see a mouse outside, will you . . .
eat him?
Um . . . I don't know if I could stop myself . . .
But what if he's the future papa of my future baby?
Oh! Then I WILL stop myself, Keshia!

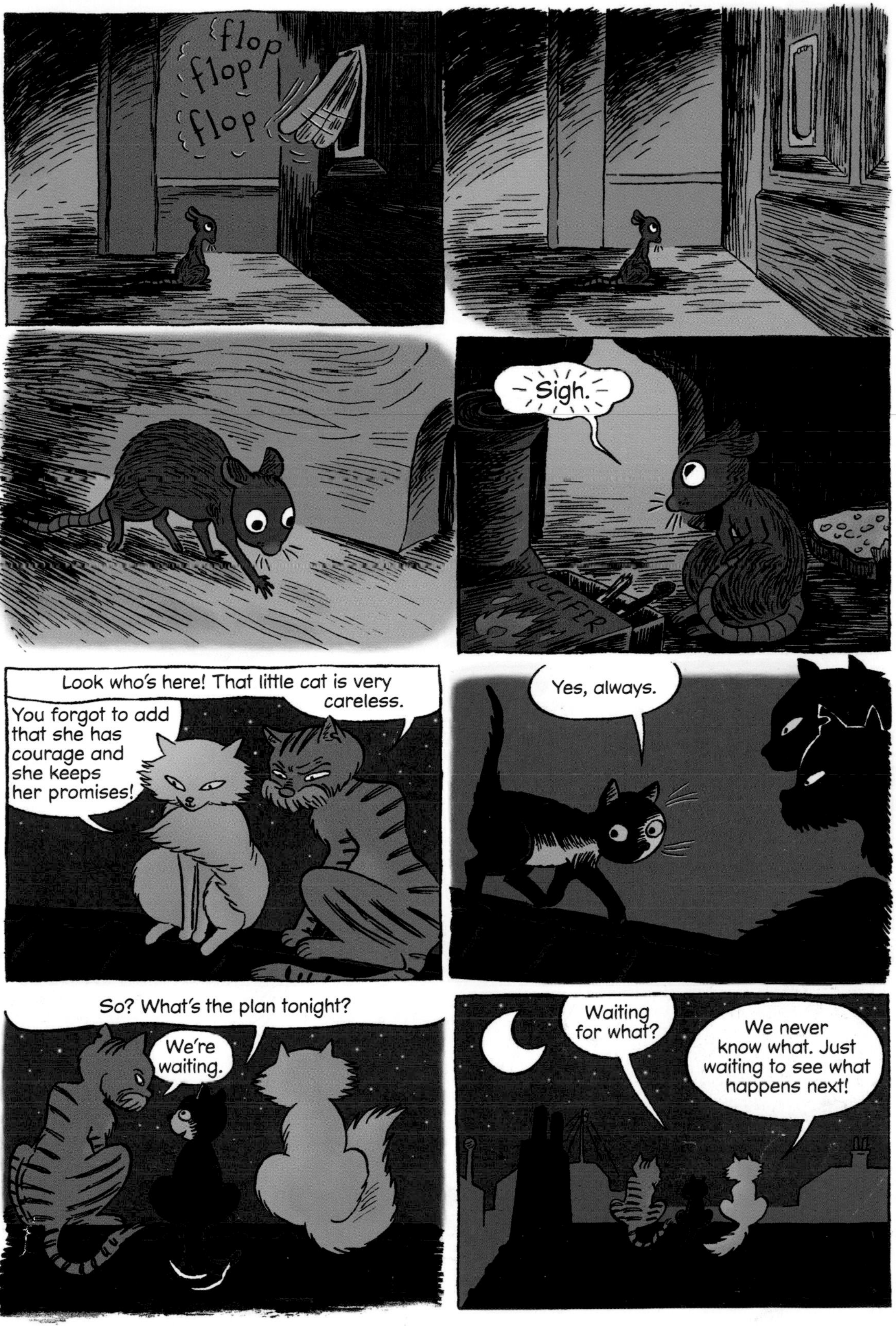
flop flop flop
Sigh.
LUCIFER
Look who's here! That little cat is very careless.
You forgot to add that she has courage and she keeps her promises!
Yes, always.
So? What's the plan tonight?
We're waiting.
Waiting for what?
We never know what. Just waiting to see what happens next!

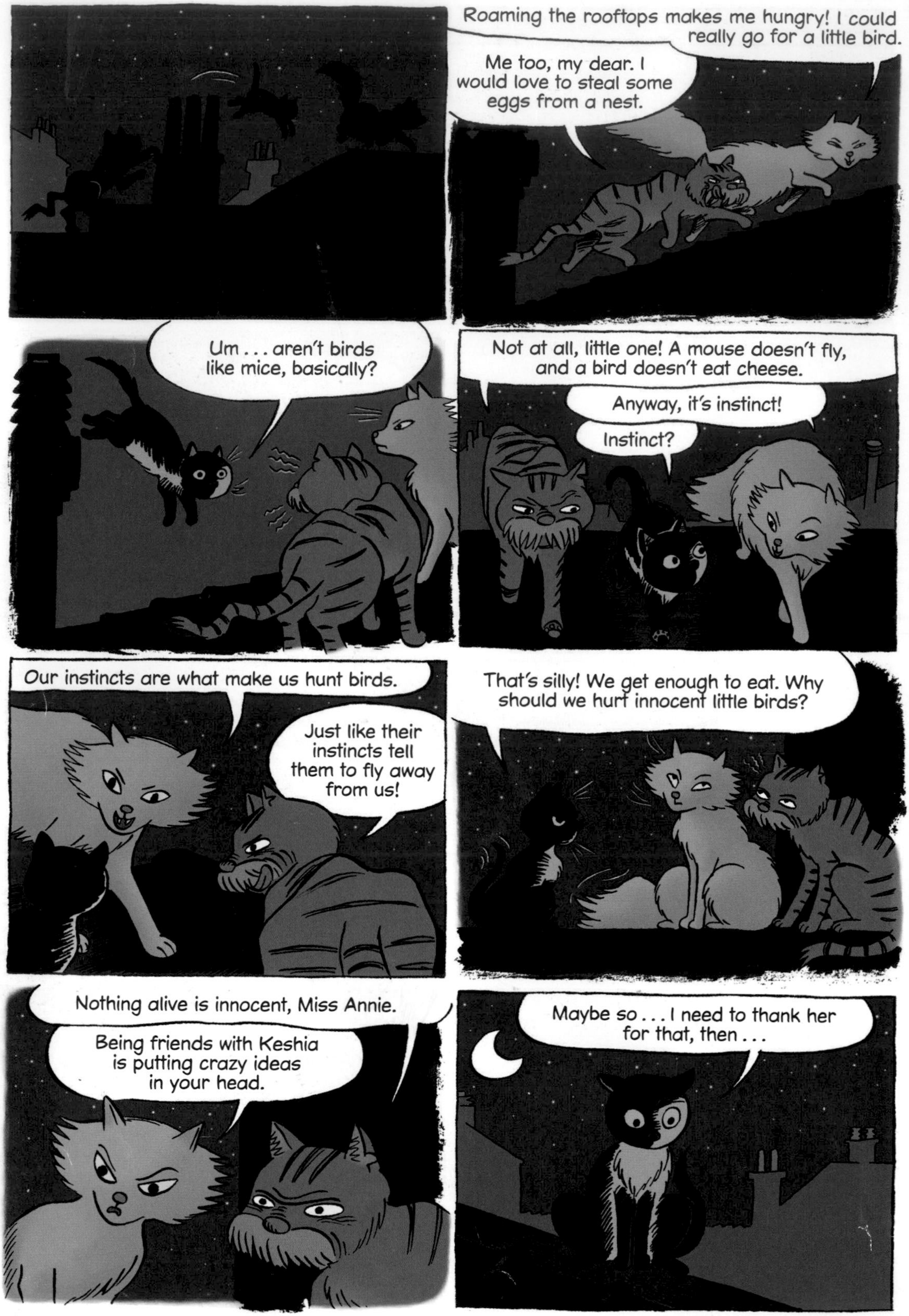
Roaming the rooftops makes me hungry! I could really go for a little bird.
Me too, my dear. I would love to steal some eggs from a nest.
Um . . . aren't birds like mice, basically?
Not at all, little one! A mouse doesn't fly, and a bird doesn't eat cheese.
Anyway, it's instinct!
Instinct?
Our instincts are what make us hunt birds.
Just like their instincts tell them to fly away from us!
That's silly! We get enough to eat. Why should we hurt innocent little birds?
Nothing alive is innocent, Miss Annie.
Being friends with Keshia is putting crazy ideas in your head.
Maybe so . . . I need to thank her for that, then . . .

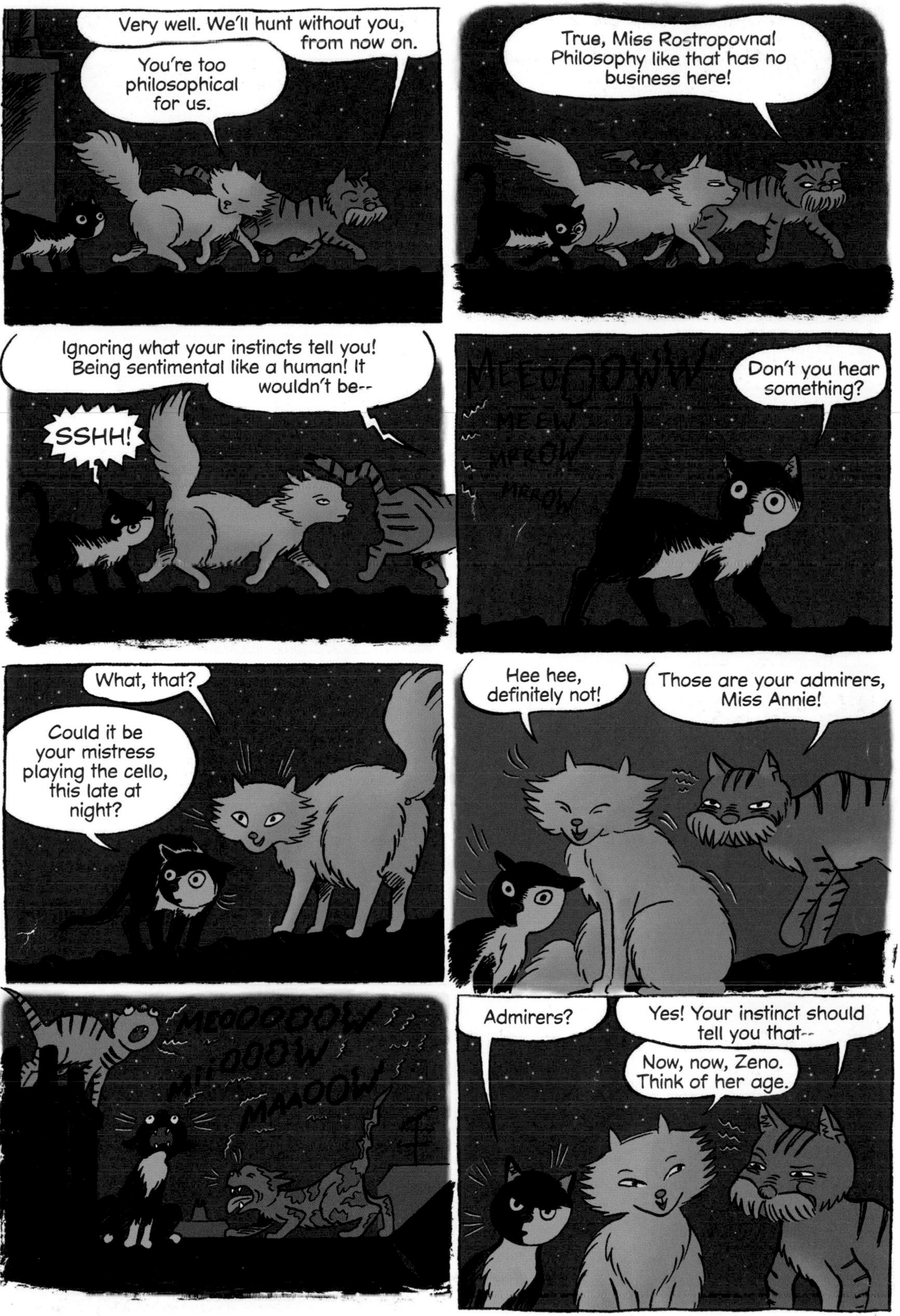

Very well. We'll hunt without you, from now on.
You're too philosophical for us.
True, Miss Rostropovna! Philosophy like that has no business here!
Ignoring what your instincts tell you! Being sentimental like a human! It wouldn't be--
SSHH!
Don't you hear something?
What, that?
Could it be your mistress playing the cello, this late at night?
Hee hee, definitely not!
Those are your admirers, Miss Annie!
Admirers?
Yes! Your instinct should tell you that--
Now, now, Zeno. Think of her age.

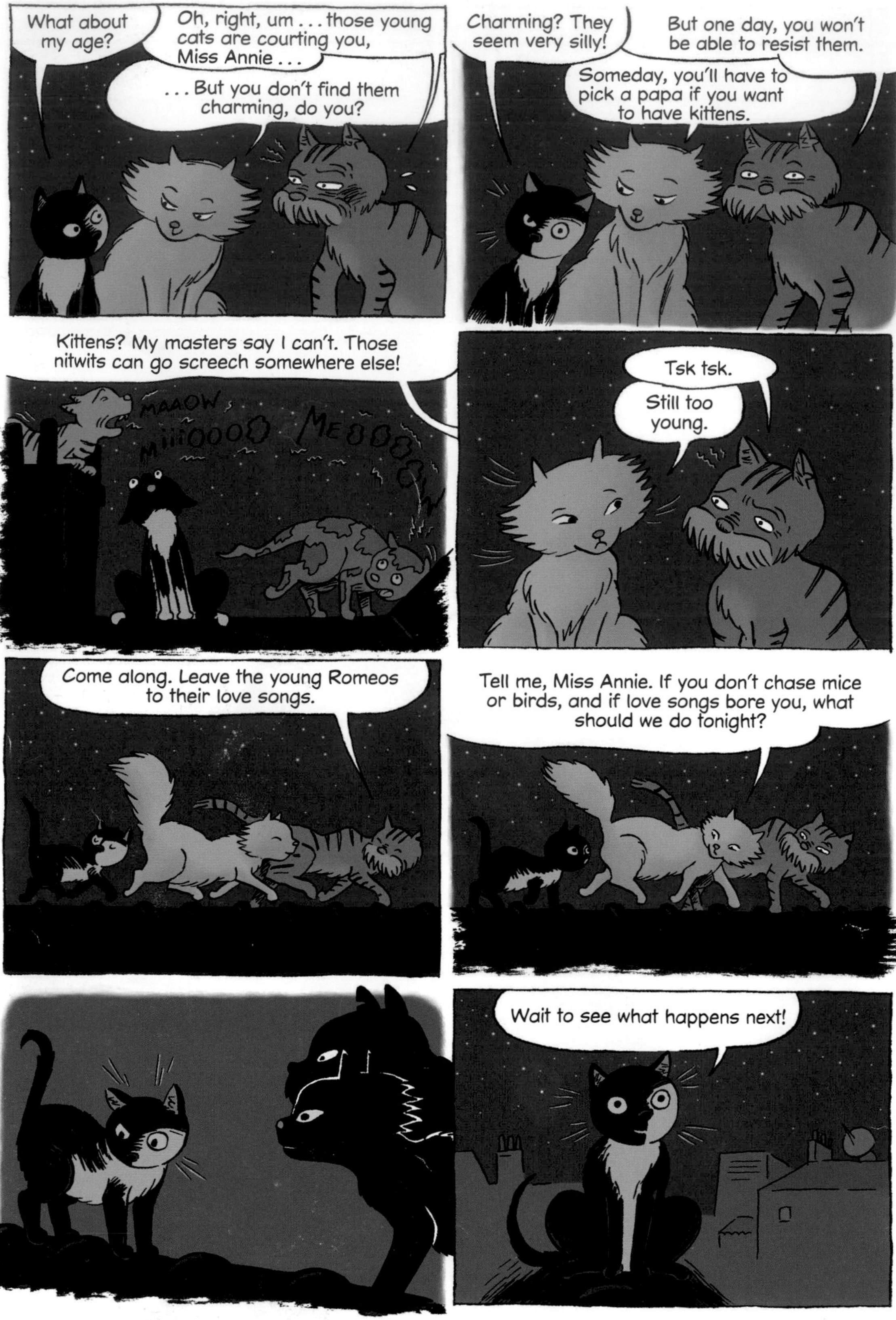
What about my age?
Oh, right, um . . . those young cats are courting you, Miss Annie . . .
. . . But you don't find them charming, do you?
Charming? They seem very silly!
But one day, you won't be able to resist them.
Someday, you'll have to pick a papa if you want to have kittens.
Kittens? My masters say I can't. Those nitwits can go screech somewhere else!
MAAOW
Miiiooooo
MEOOOOOW
Tsk tsk.
Still too young.
Come along. Leave the young Romeos to their love songs.
Tell me, Miss Annie. If you don't chase mice or birds, and if love songs bore you, what should we do tonight?
Wait to see what happens next!

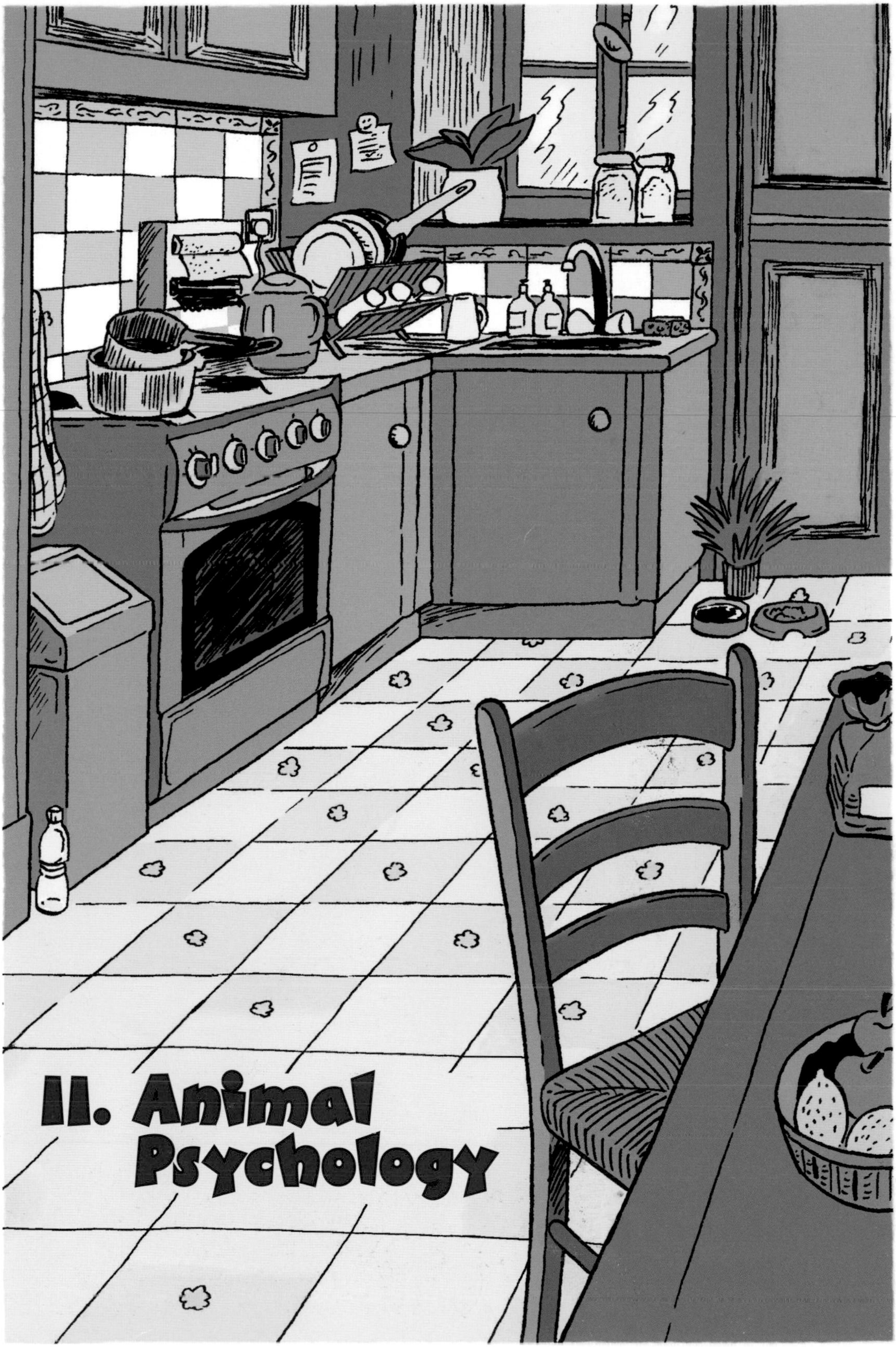

II. Animal Psychology

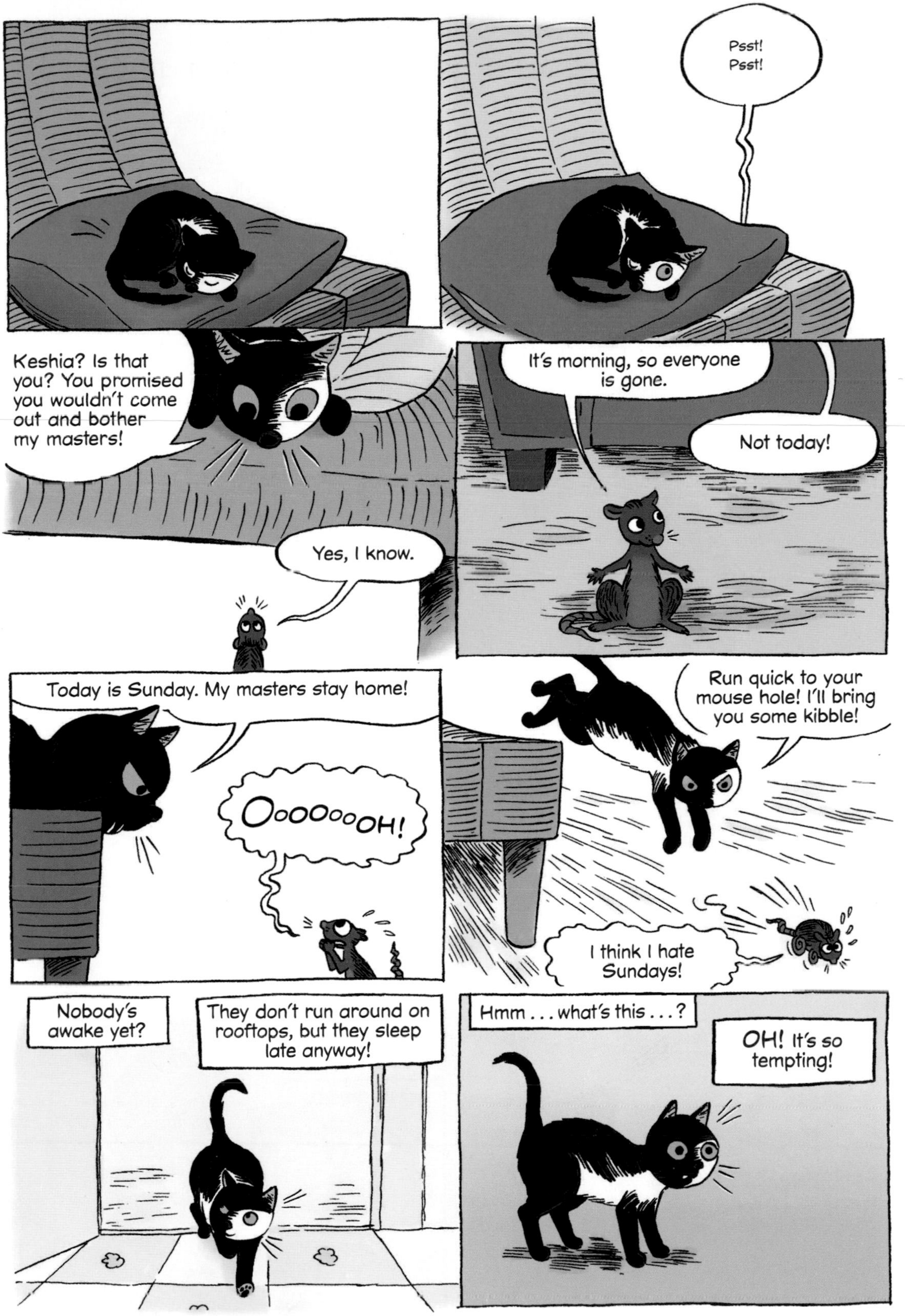
Psst!
Psst!
Keshia? Is that you? You promised you wouldn't come out and bother my masters!
It's morning, so everyone is gone.
Not today!
Yes, I know.
Today is Sunday. My masters stay home!
OoooooOH!
Run quick to your mouse hole! I'll bring you some kibble!
I think I hate Sundays!
Nobody's awake yet?
They don't run around on rooftops, but they sleep late anyway!
Hmm . . . what's this . . . ?
OH! It's so tempting!

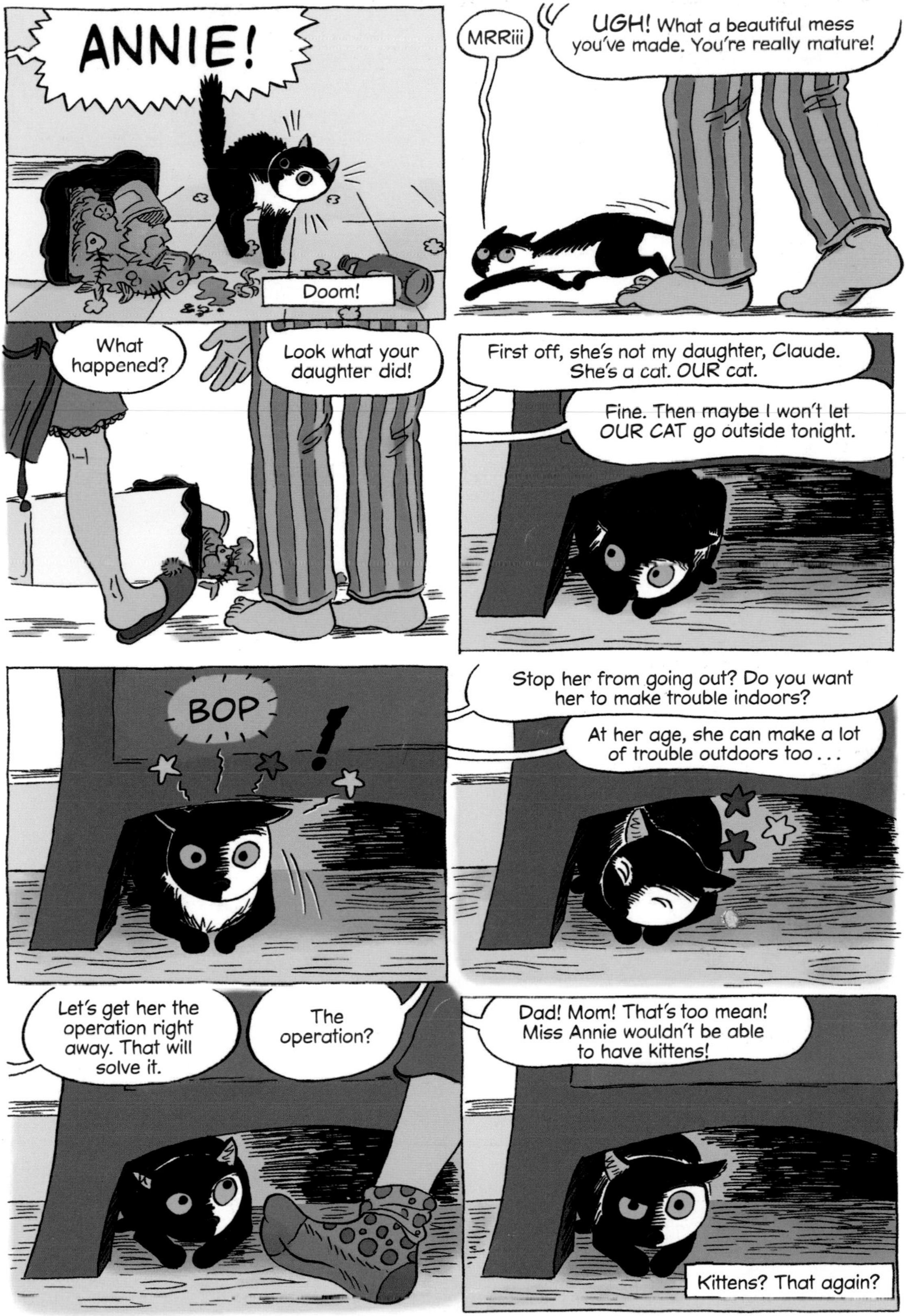
ANNIE!
Doom!
MRRiii
UGH! What a beautiful mess you've made. You're really mature!
What happened?
Look what your daughter did!
First off, she's not my daughter, Claude. She's a cat. OUR cat.
Fine. Then maybe I won't let OUR CAT go outside tonight.
BOP
Stop her from going out? Do you want her to make trouble indoors?
At her age, she can make a lot of trouble outdoors too . . .
Let's get her the operation right away. That will solve it.
The operation?
Dad! Mom! That's too mean! Miss Annie wouldn't be able to have kittens!
Kittens? That again?

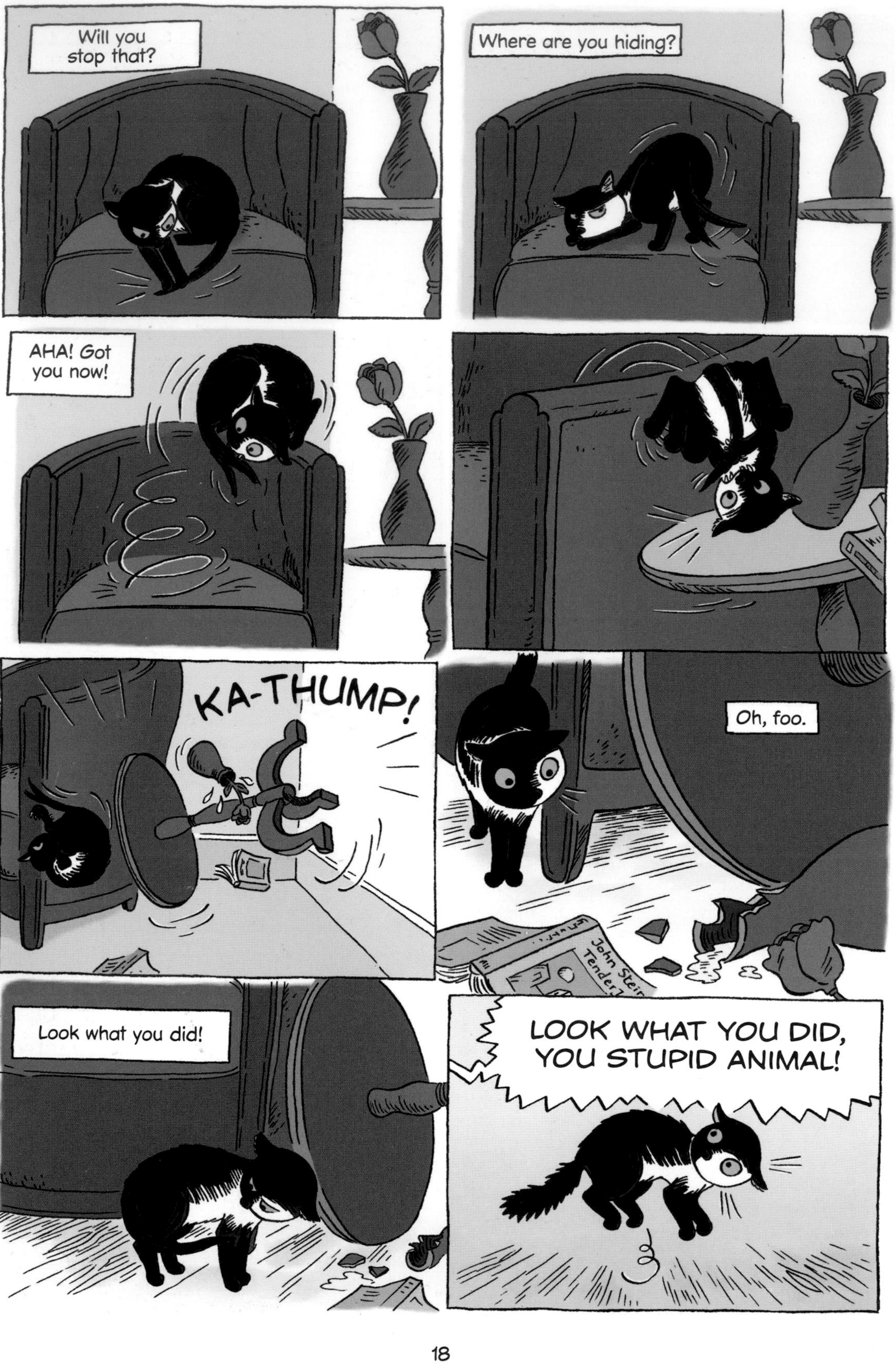
Will you stop that?
Where are you hiding?
AHA! Got you now!
KA-THUMP!
Oh, foo.
Look what you did!
LOOK WHAT YOU DID, YOU STUPID ANIMAL!

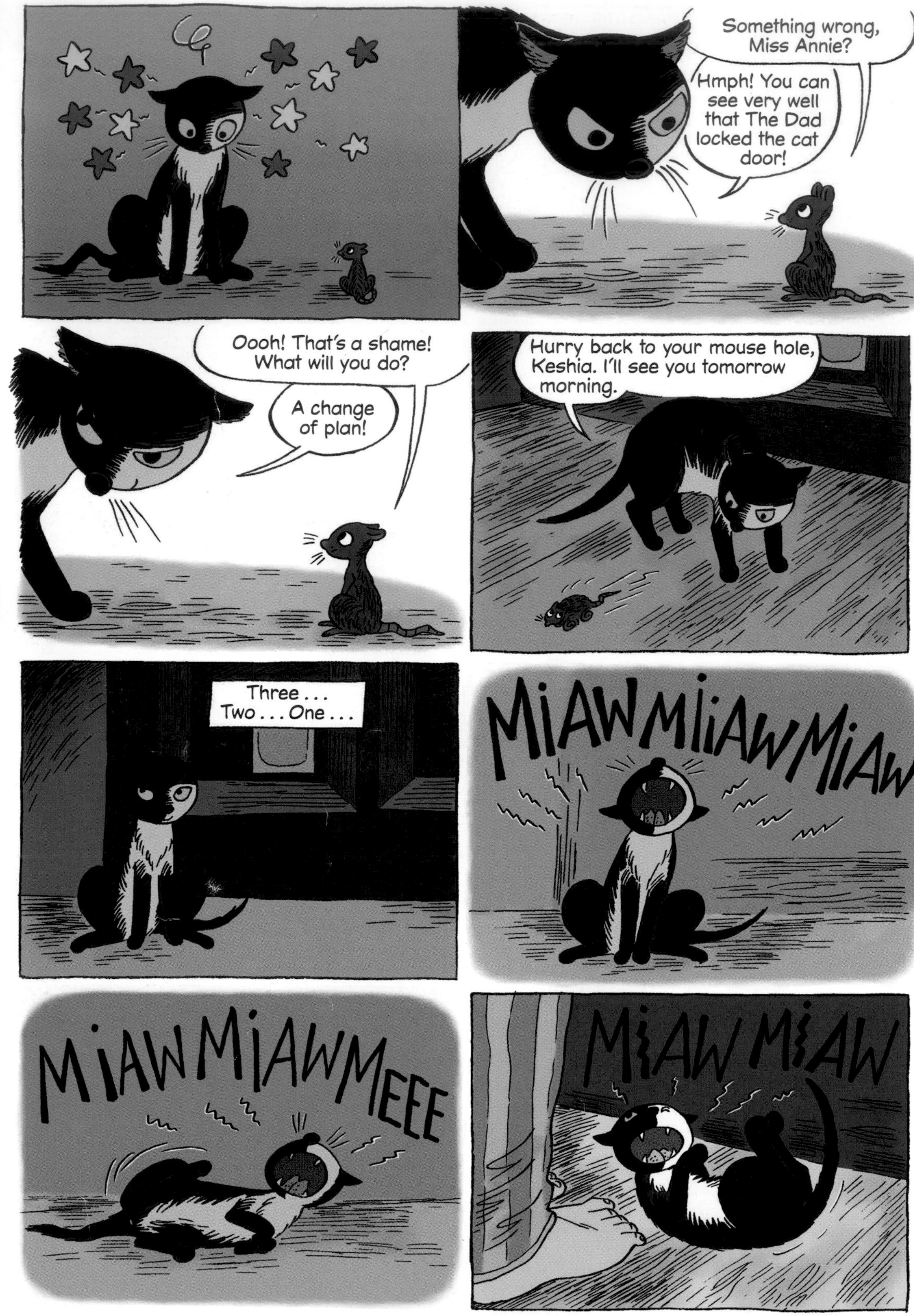
Something wrong, Miss Annie?
Hmph! You can see very well that The Dad locked the cat door!
Oooh! That's a shame! What will you do?
A change of plan!
Hurry back to your mouse hole, Keshia. I'll see you tomorrow morning.
Three . . . Two . . . One . . .
MIAW MIIAW MIAW
MIAW MIAW MEEE
MIAW MIAW

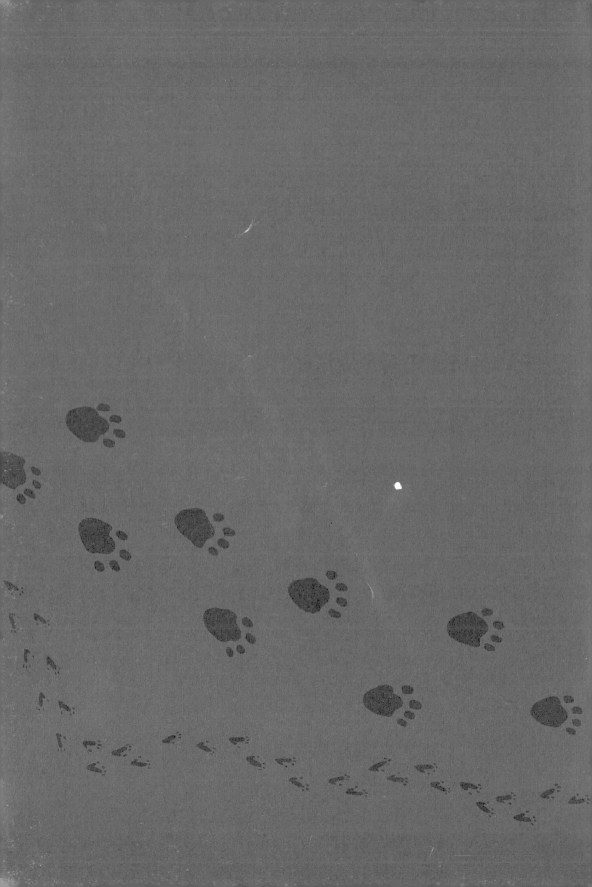

III. Zeno's Ninth Life

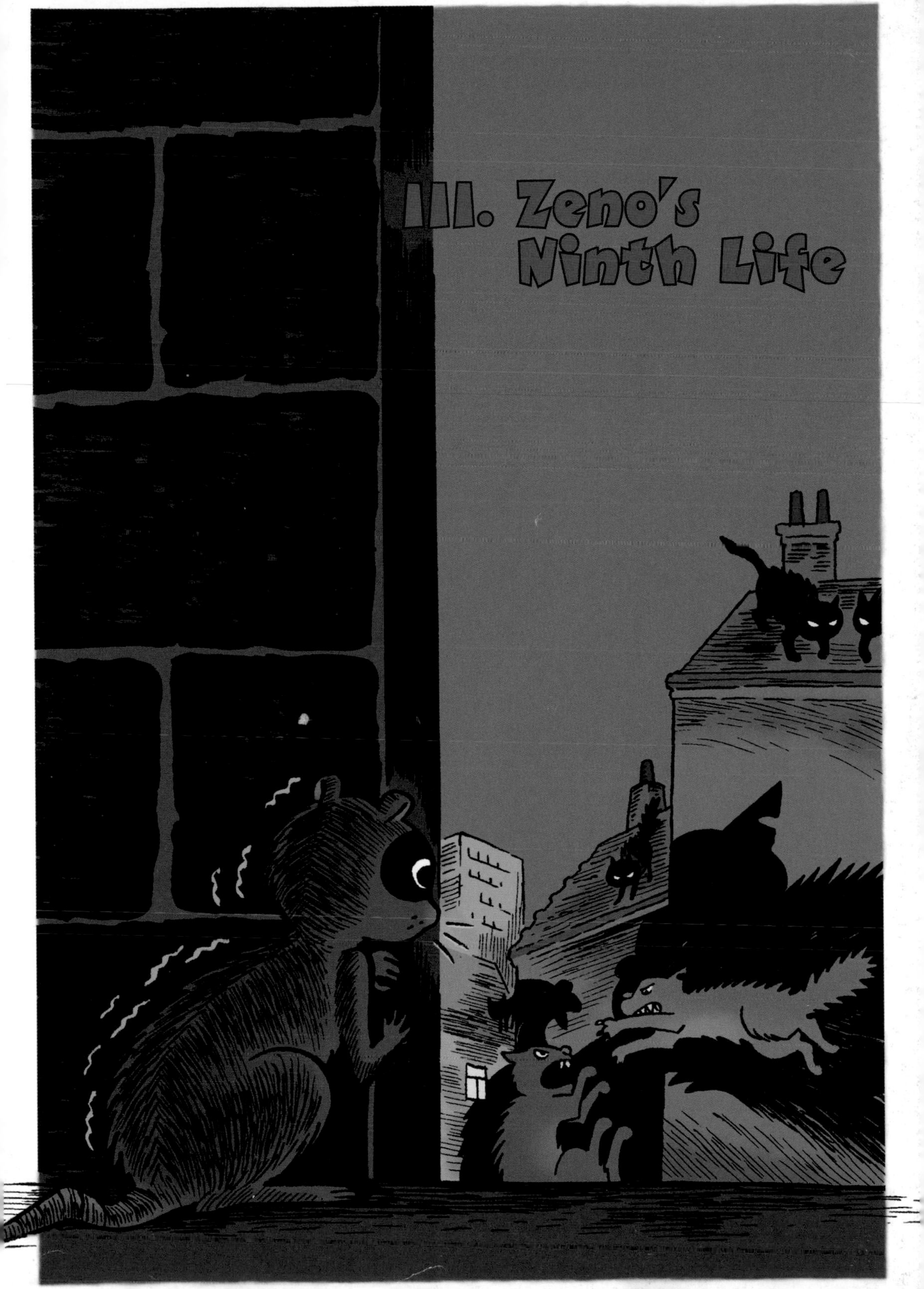

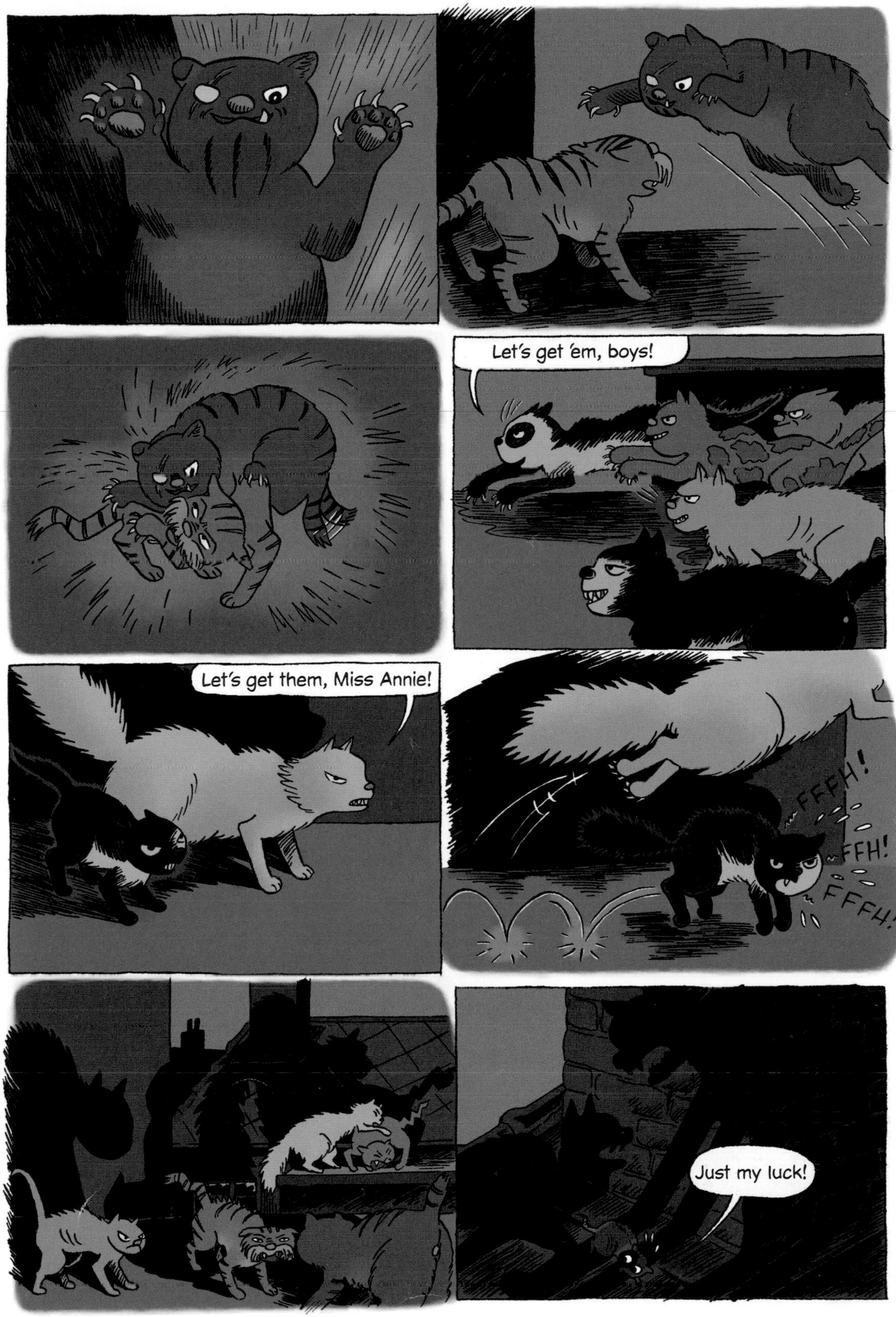
Let's get 'em, boys!
Let's get them, Miss Annie!
FFFH!
FFH!
FFFH!
Just my luck!

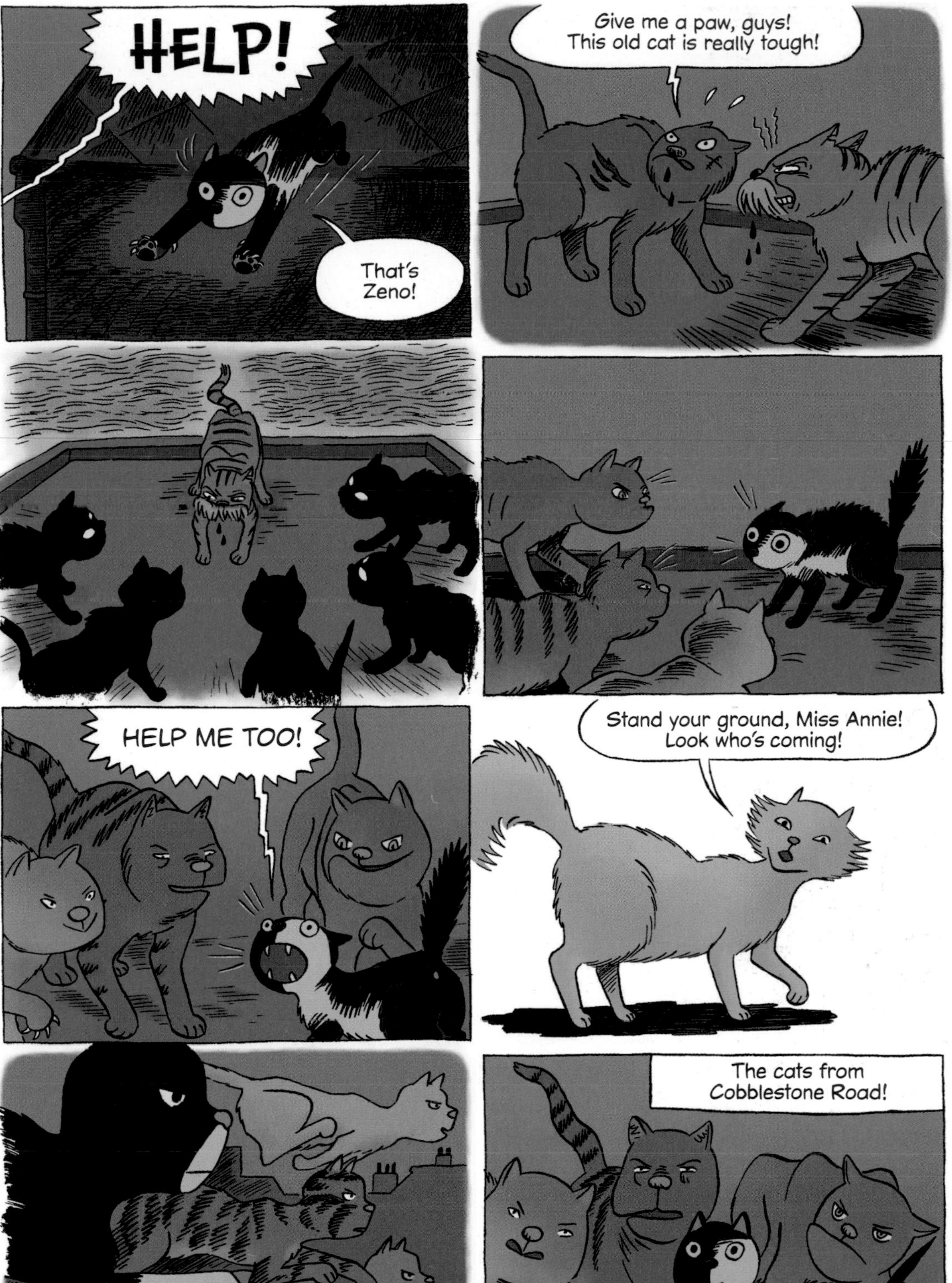
HELP!
That's Zeno!
Give me a paw, guys! This old cat is really tough!
HELP ME TOO!
Stand your ground, Miss Annie! Look who's coming!
The cats from Cobblestone Road!

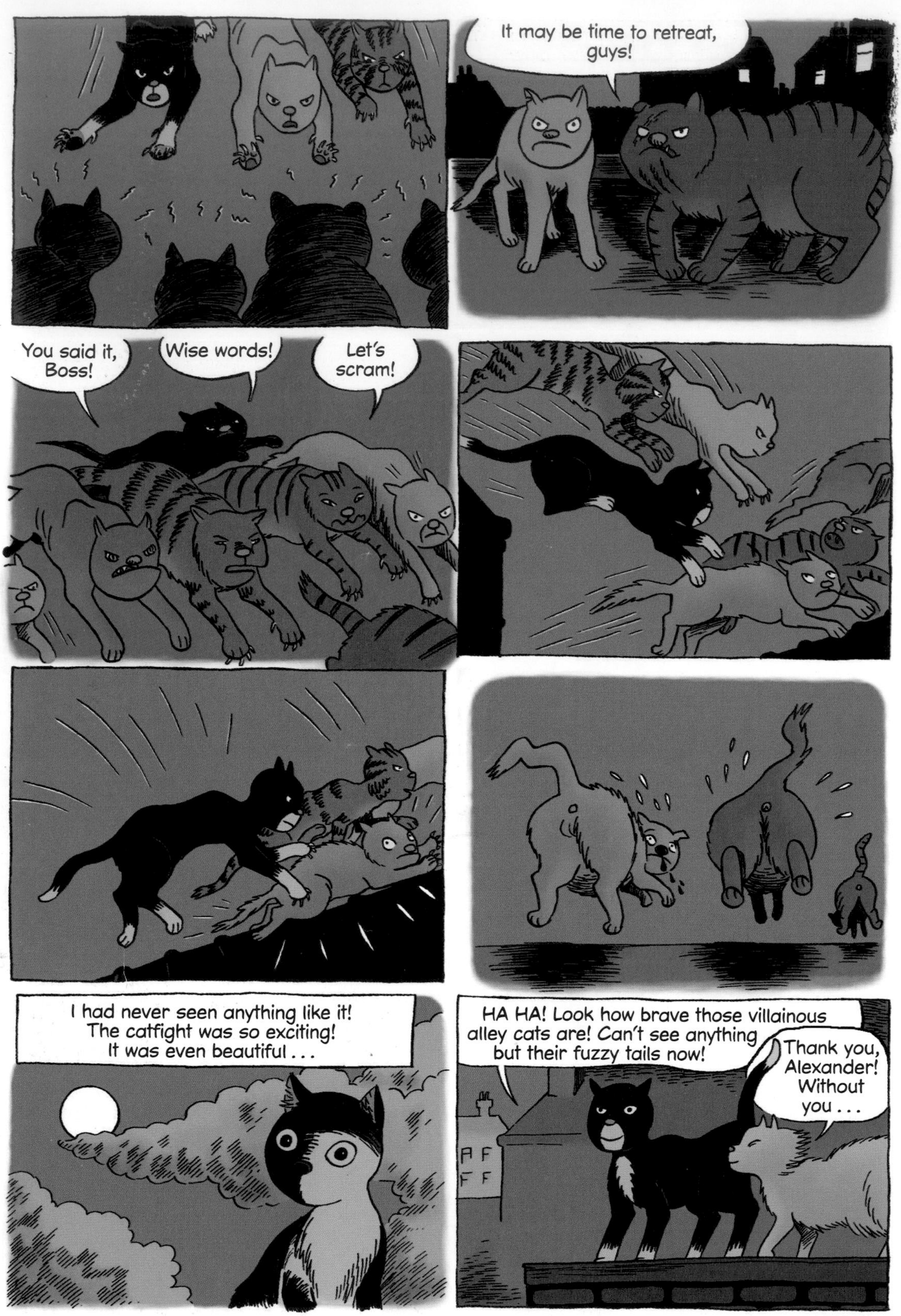
It may be time to retreat, guys!
You said it, Boss!
Wise words!
Let's scram!
I had never seen anything like it! The catfight was so exciting! It was even beautiful . . .
HA HA! Look how brave those villainous alley cats are! Can't see anything but their fuzzy tails now!
Thank you, Alexander! Without you . . .

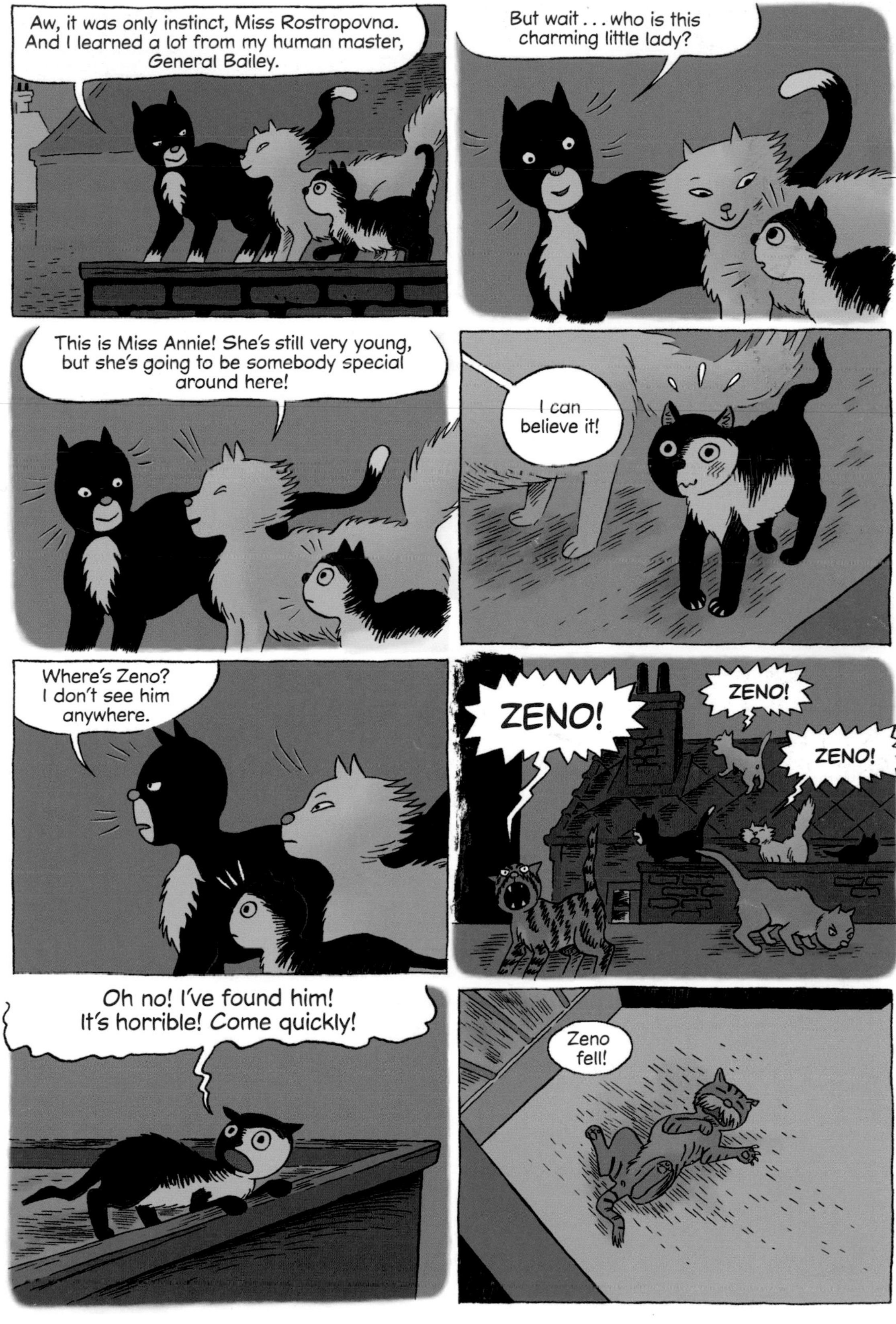

Aw, it was only instinct, Miss Rostropovna. And I learned a lot from my human master, General Bailey.
But wait . . . who is this charming little lady?
This is Miss Annie! She's still very young, but she's going to be somebody special around here!
I can believe it!
Where's Zeno? I don't see him anywhere.
ZENO!
ZENO!
ZENO!
Oh no! I've found him! It's horrible! Come quickly!
Zeno fell!

34

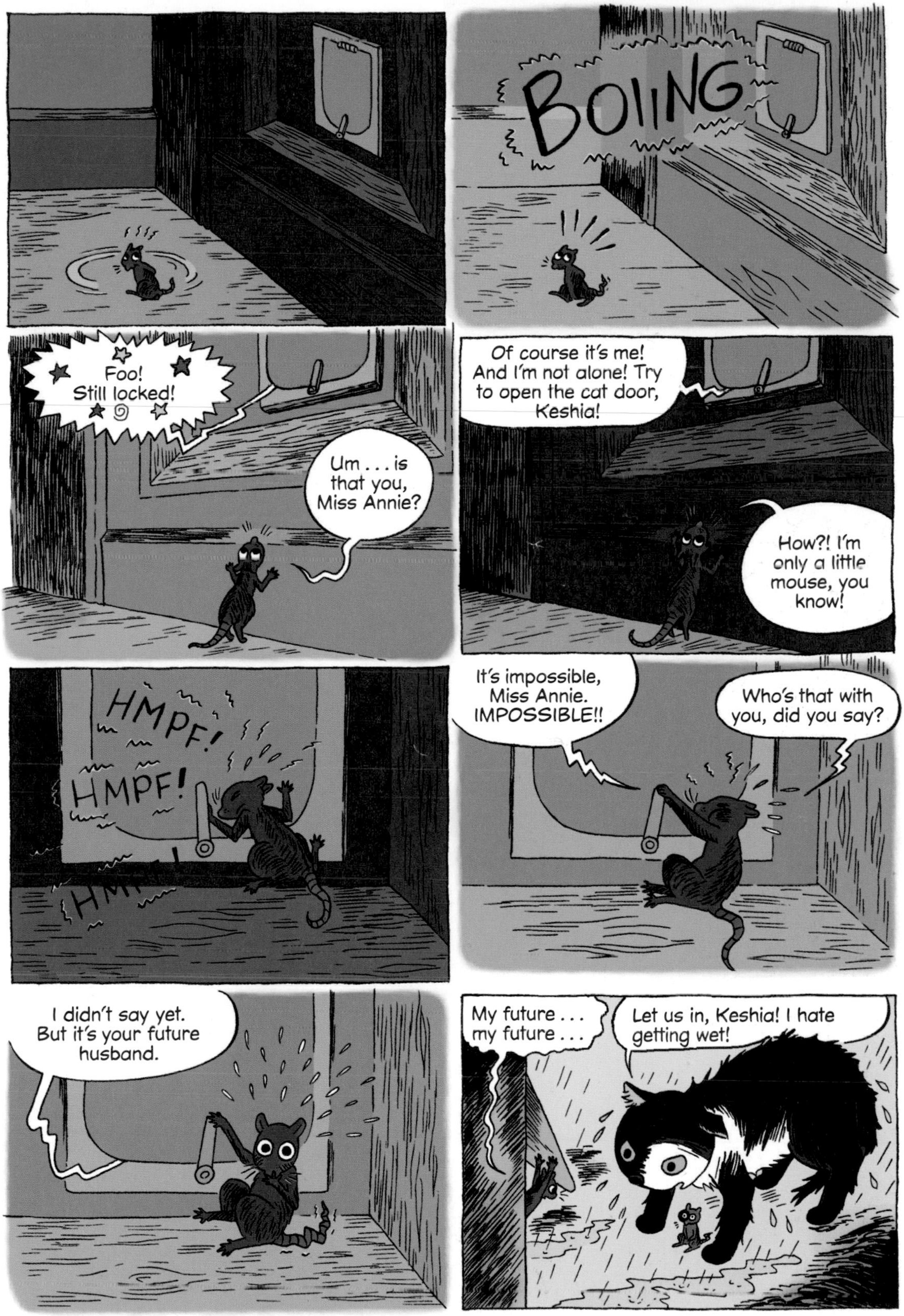
BOIING
Foo! Still locked!
Um . . . is that you, Miss Annie?
Of course it's me! And I'm not alone! Try to open the cat door, Keshia!
How?! I'm only a little mouse, you know!
HMPF!
HMPF!
It's impossible, Miss Annie. IMPOSSIBLE!!
Who's that with you, did you say?
I didn't say yet. But it's your future husband.
My future . . . my future . . .
Let us in, Keshia! I hate getting wet!

Epilogue

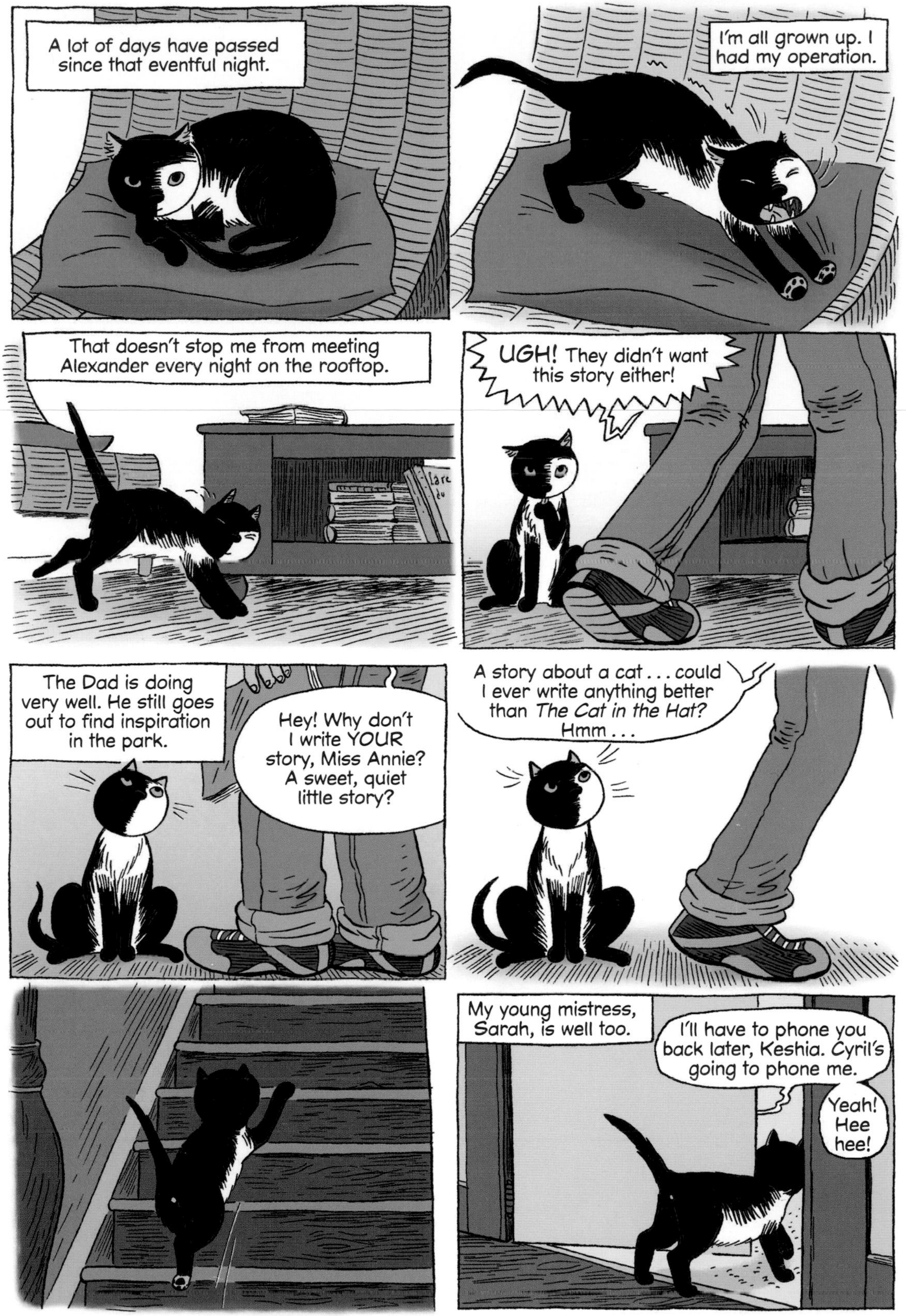
A lot of days have passed since that eventful night.
I'm all grown up. I had my operation.
That doesn't stop me from meeting Alexander every night on the rooftop.
UGH! They didn't want this story either!
The Dad is doing very well. He still goes out to find inspiration in the park.
Hey! Why don't I write YOUR story, Miss Annie? A sweet, quiet little story?
A story about a cat . . . could I ever write anything better than *The Cat in the Hat*? Hmm . . .
My young mistress, Sarah, is well too.
I'll have to phone you back later, Keshia. Cyril's going to phone me.
Yeah! Hee hee!

The End